DANGER
GUYS

Hit the
Beach

DANGER GUYS

GUYS

Hit the Beach

by Tony Abbott

illustrated by Joanne Scribner

HarperTrophy
A Division of HarperCollinsPublishers

Library of Congress Cataloging-in-Publication Data
Abbott, Tony.
    Danger guys hit the beach / by Tony Abbott ; illustrated by Joanne
Scribner.
        p.   cm.
    Summary: While spending an unexciting weekend at the beach, Noodle
and Zeek suddenly find adventure when they discover a gang of thieves
trying to steal the hidden treasure from a sunken ship.
    ISBN 0-06-440521-4 (pbk.)
    [1. Adventure and adventurers—Fiction.   2. Buried treasure—Fiction.]
I. Scribner, Joanne, ill.   II. Title.   III. Series.
PZ7.A1587Daq   1995   94-27519
[Fic]—dc20   CIP
                                                                          AC

Typography by Stefanie Rosenfeld
1   2   3   4   5   6   7   8   9   10
❖
First Harper Trophy Edition

With love for Lucy,
my littlest pal,
who keeps me young

DANGER GUYS

GUYS

Hit the
Beach

ONE

Did I say this was boring?"

That was my best friend, Zeek Pilinsky. He was leaning back on his elbows, staring out across the hot beach.

"Yeah," I said. "Twice." I was lying next to him on a beach blanket.

I had just flipped another page of *Adventure* magazine. But I wasn't really reading it anymore. I had started to doze off.

"Well, I take it back," Zeek said. "This isn't boring. This is deadly!"

I had to agree. Nothing was happening. It was all just kids with buckets, and parents talking.

"Come on, Noodle! You're the guy with all the bright ideas. You've got to think of something!"

I usually *do* think of something. I *am* the guy with all the bright ideas. That's why everybody calls me Noodle. And Zeek, he's the guy with all the muscles. That's why they call him . . . well . . . anyway, we're pretty much a team.

"Noodle, we need something *different*. Something *fun*. You know, something *exciting*!"

"Zeek," I said. "What you really mean is . . ."

"Yeah. Something DANGEROUS!"

I know how he feels. In the past couple of months, we've brushed with death no less than thirteen times. We're Danger Guys. We live the life of danger.

Well, we did. Until now.

"How about something like this?" I cracked open the magazine to a picture of two people in underwater diving suits.

"The Emersons!"

Yeah, it was Mr. and Mrs. Emerson. They were the famous husband-and-wife exploring team we had met fighting treasure thieves.

"Now *that* adventure was different, fun, exciting, *and* dangerous!" I said.

"Right. But this?" Zeek said, looking out at the water. "If this keeps up, we won't be Danger Guys anymore. We'll have to call ourselves . . ."

"Cheeseburgers?"

My dad said that. He and my mom had just come back from the snack stand with a pile of burgers, some sodas, and a few bags of chips.

"All right, Mr. Newton." Zeek laughed. "You can call us cheeseburgers, just don't call us late for lunch!" Zeek grabbed a burger right off the top and stuffed it in his mouth.

"Listen, boys," my mom said. "If you're looking for something to do, you might watch those surfers over there." She pointed down the beach to a bunch of guys with ponytails.

"I just heard them talking about something called the Golden Crest. You might ask them . . ."

Zeek grabbed my hand just as I was about to chomp my burger.

"*Golden . . . ?*" he gasped.

" *. . . Crest?*" I whispered.

"Do you think it's a ship? A *sunken* ship?"

"If there's a ship, there must be treasure! *Sunken* treasure!"

Zeek and I shot up from the sand like rockets.

"Noodle, we've got to check this out!"

"Yeah, and we've got to go under cover."

"Good call, Nood!"

We wrapped a couple of my mom's scarves around our heads like bandanas. Then we each slid on a pair of mirrored sunglasses.

"Are we cool, or are we cool!" said Zeek.

We were cool. And we were ready.

A minute later we were at the surfer camp. One of the guys was strumming a guitar. Another was playing bongos. A third was carrying a surfboard to a motor-boat sitting in the water.

Zeek nudged me. "I'm the muscle man, remember?" He flexed his arms. "Just let me do all the talking."

I nodded. Sometimes Zeek knows best. Sometimes he really surprises me. Like just now, when he walked up to the surfer with the board and started talking to him.

"Hail, surfer dude!" shouted Zeek. "Slide any choice channels lately?"

My mouth fell open. That's Zeekie—a guy of many talents.

The surfer dropped his board and hugged us. "Fellow wave dogs! People call me Boomer."

"Boomer?" I said.

"Funny, huh? Like, *boom*, suddenly

they call me that." Then he laughed. It sounded like a small explosion.

Zeek couldn't wait anymore. "So, dig that *Golden Crest*, huh?"

"Yeah! We were just going to motor out to it."

"Like, what is it?" Zeek said, nodding his head. "Spanish galleon? Dutch schooner?"

"Killer question!" said Boomer.

"I don't know, though," Zeek went on. "*Golden Crest* sounds English. A warship, maybe?"

"No, mini-dude. It's a wave!"

"Whaaa . . . ?" Zeek looked like he does when Mr. Strunk gives us homework on the weekend. His mouth hung open, and his eyes went hazy.

I tried to help him out. "You mean the Golden Crest is not a sunken treasure ship?"

"No, mini-dude! It's a wave. But what a wave! Like—*boom*—it comes from nowhere. And you ride it for miles!"

"Yeah, well, no thanks," Zeek finally said. Then he bent over to look at Boomer's surfboard.

"Where is this wave?" I asked.

"Out by the island. There." Boomer pointed out across the water to a tiny dot of land. "But you've gotta watch out for the Ugly Dude."

"Is that another wave?" Zeek snorted.

"Unh-uh! A sea monster that lives near the island. Ugly. Huge bug eyes. Big snapping claws!"

"But there aren't any sea monsters," I said.

That's when Zeek did this really dumb thing. For a guy who is so good at sports, he did something incredibly clutzy.

"Noodle," he said. "Check it out!"

I turned to see Zeek holding up Boomer's huge green surfboard. It was about ten feet tall.

"You can call me . . ." *Wham!* The board slid in the sand and slammed down on Zeek.

And on me. We both fell facedown into the motorboat with the board on top of us.

But that wasn't the worst part.

When Zeek fell on me, his foot hit this little switch on the motor.

Vrrrooom! The motor burst into life.

The propeller hit the water.

And we took off like a jet-powered racing boat.

TWO

Hey, mini-dudes! My boat! My board! Come back!"

Sure. If we could. But we couldn't.

When Zeek hit that switch on the motor, he jammed it. There was no way to stop the boat.

"Noodle! Can't you stop this boat?"

He also jammed the rudder so there was no way to steer it either.

"Can't you at least steer it?"

I was about to make a face when— *wham!*—the boat's nose bounced high off a wave.

"Whoa!" shouted Zeek. "This is like sledding on rocks!"

"Well," I snapped back. "You wanted something *different*!"

"Yeah, but . . . Noodle, watch out!"

I whirled around.

Through the spray I could see a lady on water skis. She was crossing right in front of us.

She had a really big smile until she saw us. Then her smile kind of went away. Her mouth dropped open. And she screamed.

That's when I saw the towrope.

"Duck!" I shouted to Zeek.

Vooom! Our boat shot under the towrope just in front of the lady's skis.

I looked back. The lady was still screaming.

I turned to Zeek and gave him the thumbs-up.

He usually smiles when I do that. Not this time. He had a really strange look on his face.

"NOOOOODLE!"

I turned around. A huge iron buoy

bobbled in the water just ahead. I jammed my eyes shut.

Wump! We hit a wave at incredibly the right time and incredibly the wrong way. We shot into the air and cleared the buoy by three feet.

Bam! Then we landed and really took off. Spray shot straight up on both sides of the boat. I could barely hold on. If I had eaten my cheeseburger, I sure would have lost it then.

"Okay," I yelled. "You wanted different, you got it. But it's not fun. So let's stop now, okay?"

Zeek made a face, braced himself against the side, and kicked the motor with all his strength.

Sputt! The motor died. Everything went quiet.

"Hey, I said stop it, not kill it."

Zeek shrugged and smiled. "Don't know my own strength, I guess."

"Yeah, well, great. Now how are we

going to get back?" I looked all around.

It had been a short ride, but a fast one. I couldn't even see the beach. We were drifting out to sea. The only thing anywhere near us was a small patch of land.

"Hey, what's that?" Zeek asked. "Japan?"

"Yeah, right," I said. "That must be the island Boomer was talking about. Let's swim for it."

"No thanks. I hate getting all wet, remember?"

"Oh yeah, I forgot."

"Anyway," he said, "we're better off staying in the boat. We'll be spotted sooner."

"No problem, pal," I smiled. "We'll just sit here in the . . . Say, what is the name of this boat, anyway?" I looked over the side. "Oh-oh."

"Oh-oh what?" Zeek read the name. "*Gilligan*? He named it the *Gilligan*? Oh, we're doomed. We'll be marooned here forever, eating tree bark and seaweed, while everybody else gets to go to the movies and eat cheeseburgers!"

"Hey, don't talk to me about burgers. I didn't get to eat mine, remember?"

"You can forget about lunch," Zeek said. "The next meal we'll have will be breakfast. If we're lucky."

"And don't start me thinking about— Hey, what's that?"

"What's what?"

"This water in the boat. Was it always here?"

"Water? *In* the boat? Man the lifeboat!"

"Zeek, this *is* the lifeboat. Man the surfboard!"

I tossed the board over, and we jumped on.

It was slippery. We were trying to sit up on it, when—

"*Rooaaarrr!*"

Out of nowhere rose this giant black . . . thing! It was all slimy. It had a long

snout. Huge bulging eyes. Two snaky arms
with claws on the ends of them.

"The Ugly Dude!"

The claws snapped open and shut.

They were snapping at us.

And they were getting closer.

"Paddle!" I yelled. "Fast!"

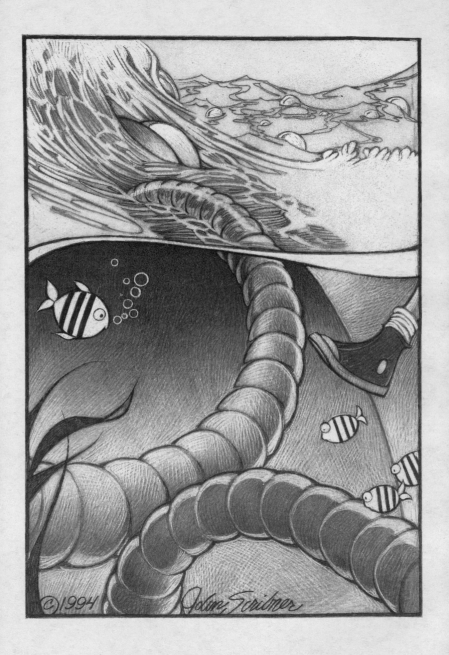

THREE

Zeek paddled with all his strength.

So did I.

Only we weren't paddling the same way.

So we didn't move.

But the sea monster did.

RRRRRRRR! The snake arms shot out again from each side of the monster's belly. They kept grabbing for us.

"Zeekie! It's going to eat us!"

Then, as if we dreamed it—*whoosh*— the monster vanished beneath the water. The air was still. It was just Zeek and me on the surfboard.

"Noodle?" Zeek said. "Have we died

and gone to surfer heaven? I mean, was there just a sea monster here? Or not?"

I looked all around. I was about to smile and give Zeek the thumbs-up, but I stopped.

Like they say, we were still in hot water.

Or at least, bubbling water.

The water began to churn all around us. It turned white and started to swell.

"Oh, no!" I cried. "The Golden Crest!"

Whoom! We were lifted up on the crest of a giant wave. It must have been thirty feet high.

The surfboard teetered at the top like a seesaw. Then the wave curled and crashed.

Shoooooom! Down we went. We hung on to the board as long as we could before it flipped over.

Wham! The board slammed into a rock, bounced up, shot back over the wave, and landed in the motorboat. Then the boat rode the wave back toward the beach where we started.

"Hey! Maybe we should have stayed—"

Wham. Wham. That's when Zeek and I hit the water. Hard.

It seemed like ten minutes before the wave threw us up on the island. And I mean *threw up! Yuck!* We were totally soaked and covered with slimy sea junk.

When we finally got to our feet, the wave was gone, and the sea was calm again.

"This is all too weird," I said.

"Yeah," Zeek said. "Like—*boom!*" He grinned and looked around. "Well, Nood, here we are, on your favorite little island. Now what?"

I scoped things out. The island was bigger than it looked at first. Beyond the beach it got pretty thick with bushes and trees. And there was a hill with a tall tree in the middle of it.

"Okay," I said, pointing up to the top. "That's where we set up camp."

"Camp? But we've got to be rescued

soon. Shouldn't we stay on the beach?"

"No way, buddy. First, the next wave might be bigger. Second, we can signal from up there. And third, don't forget about the sea monster. Maybe it's a land monster too."

Zeek didn't like that idea. "Okay, skipper," he said, trying to smile. "Let's climb."

We crossed the beach, pushed aside some branches, and walked inland. It was thick, like a jungle. And hot, too.

Big leaves flapped our faces. Long, stringy vines dangled from tall trees. We could hear these crazy, screechy birdcalls all around us.

"Can you believe it, Zeek?" I said, slapping a mosquito on my neck. "We could be a thousand miles from Mayville!"

"Yeah, trekking where no one has been before. I love it."

We wound our way through the jungle to the top of the hill. I was starting to feel like my old self again.

"Listen, Zeek," I said. "I've been thinking. Real waves don't just come from nowhere."

"Yeah, and what about real sea monsters?"

"Them either. I don't know what that thing was, but mmrrrumf . . ."

Zeek suddenly put his hand over my mouth. "Shhh!" he whispered.

We crouched on the ground. I peered through the leaves.

"Look at that," Zeek whispered. He pointed up ahead.

I followed his finger. "Zeek, it's called a tree. It's a pretty tall tree, but it's only a tree."

"No, Noodle. I mean, that!" He pointed to the trunk of the tree about ten feet up from the ground. There was a plank nailed into the trunk. Two feet above that was another plank. And then another and another, all the way to the top.

"Tree house!" I yelled.

"Mega tree house!" Zeek yelled.

FOUR

Awesome!" Zeek gasped as we scrambled up onto a platform in the tree house. "Just look at this setup. I could live here forever."

It was cool, for sure.

We stood in a little room. In the middle was a table made from a small door. A hammock of leaves and vines hung in the corner.

"Nobody has lived here for a long time," I said, looking around the room.

Zeek stepped over and swung himself onto the hammock. *Wump!* It collapsed on the floor.

"Hey, be careful. This stuff is way old.

The whole place might fall apart with us in it." I wiped a thick layer of gunk from the table.

"Let's explore the rest," Zeek said.

A winding set of stairs ran around the tree up to another level. I tested the stairs. They wobbled a little, but we went up anyway.

We stepped out on an open deck. It had a seat and a shelf built into the tree.

"Cool. This could be your station, Noodle. It's even got a place to put your books."

"Great, Zeek," I said, looking over the side to the jungle way down below. "But let's think about making a signal now."

"Yeah, in a minute. I bet the real exciting stuff goes on up there!" Zeek pointed up to the top level. It was twenty feet higher up the tree, and the only way to get there was a skinny rope ladder.

"Um . . . Zeek?" I gulped. "There's something I never really told you."

"Yeah? What's that, buddy?"

"I don't like going too high. I keep thinking I'm going to fall. Sorry, I know it's pretty bad for a Danger Guy, but . . ."

"Hey, no problem," Zeek said. "There are things I don't like. But that's why we're such a great team. Between us, we can do everything."

Zeek smiled and slapped me on the back. "Come on, buddy, let's go up. I'll keep you safe." The rope swung back and forth as we climbed. It made me kind of sick.

Finally we reached the top platform.

Then we saw it.

"Holy cow!" I gasped. "It's Mayville! You can see the entire coast from here!"

The view was unbelievable. Across the wide blue water was our town. The beach, the mall, everything.

"Right," Zeek said. "And just look at this."

He pointed to the roof over the platform. It was a piece of ship's sail tied to some branches with strips of vine. "A shade roof. Isn't this neat? I mean, who made this incredible tree house?"

We didn't have to look far for an answer. On the floor was an old wooden chest. There were some words carved on the outside. I brushed the carving with my hand.

"It says, 'Captain John May, 1785.'"

"May? May!" Zeek looked at me. "You mean *May*, as in *Mayville*?"

"I can't believe it! He was shipwrecked, remember? Mr. Strunk told us that in class. He must have been marooned right here!"

"Cool! And he probably looked over there and said, 'Someday they'll call that Mayville!'"

"Something like that," I said. I went to open the chest.

"Wait a second, Noodle." Zeek put his hand on the chest. "Maybe we shouldn't. I saw this movie once where they put a guy . . ."

"Look, it's a treasure chest, right? It's

28

probably full of gold. It's got to be."

"Or maybe it's full of bones. Maybe the guy who built this tree house is in there, all rotten."

I didn't say anything. I just wiped away the dust and waited.

Then Zeek leaned over my shoulder. "Well, come on. Are you going to do it, or not?"

I smiled and opened the chest.

But then Zeek did it again. Clutzy thing number two.

He stuck his head right into the opening. He screamed. And he jumped back into me.

I tumbled backward. My arms went flying. I grabbed on to the roof branches to catch my balance.

Zeek grabbed on to me.

The vines holding the roof snapped.

The roof slid off.

And we went with it.

FIVE

It was him! It was him! I saw him, the dead guy, in the box. It was horrible!"

Zeek didn't get it.

Not right away.

It took him a second. Then he went quiet.

And he looked down.

"Noodle?" he said quietly. "We're not in the tree house anymore, are we?"

Bingo! He finally got it.

But I didn't answer him. I was too busy trying to hold on to the tree house roof. Just why I was holding on to it, I didn't know. It made us fall even faster.

"We're falling, and we're going to die!" I screamed.

Suddenly, the sail in the roof puffed up with air. Hot ocean air. We stopped falling so fast. In fact, we stopped falling at all.

The sail caught a breeze and pulled us up. We soared around the tree and up to the left.

"Hey, we're hang gliding!" I cried.

"You're gliding, I'm hanging! Pull it up, Noodle!"

I looked down. Zeek was hugging my knees. His feet were kicking through the treetops as we drifted over them.

"Hey," I called down to him. "You think I like this? I told you I don't like heights. We wouldn't even be here if you hadn't . . ."

Then he started to wiggle.

"Don't do that!" I cried.

"I can't *not* do it! I'll fall if I don't do it! Help! Noodle, I'm slipping!"

Zeek slid down to my ankles.

"Just don't grab my sneakers," I yelled.

"The laces aren't—whoa!"

The wind caught us again, and we sailed clear up over the island.

That's when I saw it.

"Zeekie! Look!"

There, under the blue water, about a hundred feet below the surface, was a long, dark shadow.

Even from way up there I knew what it was.

"Zeek! It's a ship! It's Captain May's ship! We found it. We found it!"

"Uh-huh. That's nice," Zeek squeaked. He was still wiggling at my ankles.

But that wasn't the only thing I saw. There was a campfire smoking on the beach below. And in a cove nearby, some men were moving around. Some of them had scuba diving gear on.

And not only that. A high-powered motorboat came growling into the cove.

Whoosh! A quick breeze pushed us back around and over the trees.

"I knew it, Zeek! I knew something cool

would happen. You just have to wait. Talk about different! This is different, all right. It might even be scary, even though scary is not on your list."

"Noodle? We're flying a little low."

"And of course, you can't really scare Danger Guys. No way."

"Watch where you're going, okay?"

"But it might even be getting a little fun. I think it's getting fun. Do you think it's getting fun?"

"Noodle, pull it up!"

"Listen, Zeek. It's pretty clear what we have to do. Those guys are up to no good. And we've got to—"

"NOOOOOODLE!"

SIX

W*ham!*

We hit a tree.

Wham!

We hit another tree.

Wham!

We hit a third tree, I let go of the sail, and we dropped like a sack of stones.

The last thing I saw as I looked up was the sail gliding on over the treetops.

We ripped down through the tree branches and landed headfirst in a bush.

I stood up. Zeek stood up right next to me. He looked okay, but then he did something weird.

"Noodle! Where are you?" he yelled,

as if I were a mile away.

"Right here. Where do you think?"

He turned and looked straight into my face. "Whoa!" he said. "I didn't see you!" Then he started to crack up.

"What's so funny?"

"You! Jungle Man!"

I looked down. It was true. Big leaves, vines, and branches were sticking out of my shorts, through my hair, and in my socks. I was totally camouflaged!

"Yeah, it's the latest." I went to pull off the junk.

"No," said Zeek. "Keep it on! We can sneak up on these guys, and they won't even see us."

Then Zeek ripped some leaves off the bush he was standing in. He jammed them into his shirt.

"Okay, now we're ready!"

"Not quite," I said. I picked up a handful of dirt and smeared Zeek's face with it.

"Commandos!" I said.

Then Zeek smeared me.

"Hey, pal," I said. "Is it fun yet?"

"Yeah," said Zeek. "It's getting there."

Slowly we made our way down to the beach. We didn't make a sound. When we passed by, not even a leaf moved. We were good.

Then I froze. I held up my hand.

The camp was just a few feet away. The motorboat was moored in the cove nearby.

I looked around. Three men were moving crates and underwater equipment to the boat.

I nodded at Zeek. He nodded back.

We moved up slowly. We stood right next to a leafy tree, held our breaths, and listened.

One big guy with silver hair picked up a crate near the campfire. He sang a song as he brought it over to the boat.

> *"Many brave hearts are asleep*
> *In the Deep.*
> *So, beware!"*

A man with a little thin mustache stopped what he was doing and stared at the first guy.

"Stop it. You know this island is haunted."

"Beware!" the other man sang again. Then he laughed.

"Well, there *is* a ghost," Mustache said. "And he's angry we're messing around with his treasure. Heck, I feel like someone's watching us right now!"

I nudged Zeek. It was hard not to smile.

Just then, a strange shadow passed over the camp. It was gone in a second.

"Wooooooo!" said the first man, laughing. "Maybe that was your ghost!"

"Shut up, both of you!" grunted a heavy bald guy in scuba gear. "Here comes the Boss!"

Suddenly, they all started hustling around. The Boss was walking up the beach.

I expected a big ugly guy with a scar on his face.

I was wrong. The Boss wasn't big. The Boss wasn't ugly. And the Boss wasn't a guy!

The Boss was a woman. She looked like a TV actress, with lots of big blond hair. She wore black scuba gear with red stripes up the sides.

"Get to work, you bums!" she growled. "This whole place goes up in an hour!"

"Goes up?" Zeek whispered. "What does she mean *goes up*?"

I shrugged my branches.

The Boss pulled something from a little pack she had. "I'll find more of these if I have to blast that wreck to smithereens!"

Then she tossed the thing onto a crate. It spun there for a second then flattened. I squinted through my leaves.

"GOLD! Zeek! Look! A gold coin! I knew it! I told you there was treasure!"

Suddenly, things got very quiet. Everyone looked over at where I was standing.

"Hey!" shouted the bald guy. "Did that tree say something?"

Zeek tore off into the bushes.

"It's the ghost!" Mustache cried.

But the silver-haired guy knew better. Before I could move an inch, he had leaped over the campfire and grabbed me.

Suddenly, some kind of big round nut dropped from the tree.

Bonk!

The guy stopped pulling. He smiled at me. Then his eyes closed. And he fell backward.

"Way to go, Zeekman!" I yelled out.

I was about to dash into the jungle when I heard the leaves rustling above me. I looked up.

Bonk!

The last thing I heard was Zeek saying something like "Sorry, Noodle!"

Then everything went dark.

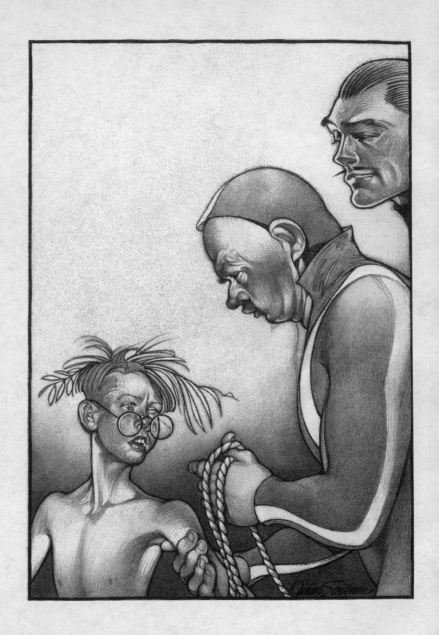

SEVEN

When I woke up, there was a plate of steaming, hot waffles in front of me. My favorite food! I could smell the butter melting.

Someone was pouring syrup on the waffles and handing me a fork.

Only I couldn't move my hands. I tugged and tugged but I couldn't get at those waffles.

That's when I really woke up.

The waffles disappeared right away. And the smell wasn't butter, but something stinky burning on the campfire.

I couldn't move my hands because they

were tied. My head hurt, too. And boy, was I hungry!

But first things first.

I looked around. Zeek wasn't anywhere. But everybody else was. Maybe they would just take their gold and go.

That's when the Boss said something that sent chills up my spine.

"No more little blasts, you guys. I want another five hundred pounds of dynamite in that wreck. Let's blow that old hulk out of the water now!"

"But . . ." the mustache guy said. "Five hundred pounds? That will make a blast so big . . . it'll cause a tidal wave!"

So that's it! Suddenly all the pieces fit.

The big Golden Crest waves were caused by underwater explosions. But they'd be like bathtub splashes next to the blast she was talking about.

"So what!" the Boss snapped back. "*Ka-boom!* One little town on the coast gets washed away. Who cares?"

I couldn't take it. "I care, lady!" I

shouted at her. "And Zeek cares too! Gold doesn't mean anything when people's lives are at stake!"

I tried to wiggle free, but the knots were tight.

"Shut up, small fry," the Boss growled at me. "Or your next word will be your last." Then she tossed a nasty looking black dart gun over to Mustache. It was the kind divers use to protect themselves from sharks. "Shoot him with a stun dart if he tries anything funny."

The Boss walked over to the boat with the other two men. That left Mustache keeping his eye on me.

This little adventure had just turned serious.

Then I got an idea.

"Hey," I said to Mustache. "You're right about that ghost. I saw him too. Big guy. Ugly. With a skull for a head."

"Aw, don't talk about it. Or do I have to tie up your mouth, too?"

Good. It was working. I was trying to

scare him so he'd make a mistake. Then I'd run for it. "Slimy eyeballs! And creepy bloody—!"

"Aaaaaaeeee!" A horrible cry echoed through the cove.

Everybody looked up.

"Aaaaaaeeee!"

There, on the cliff above the cove, stood a ghostly figure. It looked like a skeleton with creepy old clothes hanging off it. And it had a huge sword in its hand!

"The ghost!" Mustache yelled. He took off for the boat.

I wanted to do the same thing. That ghost was right out of the kind of horror movie I'm not allowed to watch!

But I couldn't get up.

"Aaaaaaeeee!"

Everybody picked up their underwater stun guns and started firing at the ghost.

Fwing! Zing!

The ghost struck quickly. It leaped off the cliff, its giant cutlass flashing.

Plonk! Silver-Hair's stun gun went flying.

Pwing!-splash! Baldy dove face first in the sand as the ghost knocked his gun into the water.

"Aaaaaaeeee!" the ghost screamed its ugly scream again. My blood ran cold.

It swooped down on me now. I couldn't move. It raised the gigantic sword.

I shut my eyes.

Chomp!

EIGHT

The blade flashed down inches from my neck.

It missed me.

But suddenly, my hands were free. I tried to run before the ghost hacked me for real.

Too late. It grabbed me and pulled me up into the air. It stuck its creepy mouth in my ear. It spoke to me.

"Noodle! You okay?"

"Zeekie!" I yelled. "It's you ! It's—! But how did you—? I mean, where did you—?"

Whoom! The vine we were swinging on pulled tight, and we started to swoop back up to the cliff.

"The chest in the tree house!" Zeek shouted. "It wasn't a dead guy, it was his clothes!"

Suddenly, the motorboat roared into life.

My brain worked lightning fast. I had to tell Zeek everything I knew in a split second. But all that came out was: "Dynamite! Explosion! Tidal wave! MAYVILLE!"

I grabbed Zeek's huge sword from him. I aimed it at the vine just above us.

"Noodle? What are you doing? Noodle!"
Chomp!

Zeek looked at me as we fell. His mouth opened wide. He screamed.

But I think he understood.

Wump! Wump! I had timed it perfectly. We fell right into the boat, just as the Boss steered it out of the cove.

Zeek in his yucky old ghost clothes dropped right on Mustache. The guy freaked. Then he fainted.

I landed on Silver-Hair and knocked him over.

"Quick!" yelled Zeek as Baldy came for him. "What's the plan?"

"Part One!" I yelled, tossing the sword back to him. "You hold them off while I grab some scuba gear!"

He made a face, but swung the cutlass, and Baldy backed away. That gave me time to grab two masks, a couple of oxygen tanks, and some flippers.

"Part Two. We dive!"

Then that dark shadow passed overhead. Baldy and the Boss looked up.

Splash! We disappeared into the water before they knew it. The boat tore off toward the wreck.

We swam to shore dragging the scuba gear.

"Quick," I said. "Suit up before they blast."

The flipper feet were big on us, but we strapped them tight. Then we pulled on the heavy oxygen tanks.

"Wait a minute," said Zeek. "What am I doing? I barely remember how any of this stuff works. Besides, I *really* hate to get wet, remember?"

I looked at Zeek and patted him on the back. "Trust me on this one, pal." I sucked on the spout that came from the mouthpiece. "You just do this. Remember?" I had dragged Zeek to scuba lessons a couple of summers ago.

He took a quick breath and smiled. "Oh, yeah. It's all coming back to me."

"And another thing," I said. "If something cool happens down there, don't give me the thumbs-up."

"Um . . . Give me a hint . . ."

"Because underwater, thumbs up means to go to the surface. Do this instead." I made a circle with my thumb and forefinger and stuck my other fingers straight up. "This is the okay sign."

"Cool. The bunny sign."

"Very funny. And this," I said, running my finger across my throat, "means . . . "

"Something uncool. I remember already," Zeek said. "Noodle, wait. What's the plan?"

The truth? I didn't have a plan. And Zeek wouldn't go for something dumb like Stop Those Bombers!

So I just smiled a big smile, snapped my face mask down, gave Zeek the new okay sign, and dove out into deep water.

A second later he was beside me. Yeah, I guess we're a team, no matter what.

It was a whole different world down there. The water was warm and green. Blue light rippled through it. It was beautiful, all right.

Then there it was, dead ahead. The wreck.

The long wooden ship was lying on its side. The hull was still together. Old ghostly rigging hung off the mast and quivered in the water.

Then we froze. The motorboat roared just above us. The motor shut off.

Three splashes. The Boss, Baldy, and Silver-Hair all dove in. They carried a black bundle.

Dynamite!

Maybe they won't see us, I thought.

Fwing! A stun dart whizzed by my face mask!

Okay, so they saw us! We took off into the wreck. It was cramped and creepy in there. We swam up stairways and through hatches, paddling our flippers as fast as we could.

But Baldy was after us as though he had a motor strapped on him.

We just managed to escape out a tiny hole when everything went white with light. And two giant eyeballs glared at us from the depths.

The sea monster!

It shot up from the shadows.

Zeek looked at me with wide eyes and started for the surface.

He didn't make it. A huge snakelike arm snapped out and grabbed his leg in its claw.

Clamp! Now it had me by the leg.

It was pulling us down.

I caught a last glimpse of Zeek as the shadows closed on him.

He was running his finger slowly across his throat.

John Scribner ©94.

NINE

Zeekie!" I bubbled.

The monster's slimy arms dragged us down under its belly. We were locked tight in the grip of its claws.

Down we went.

I was waiting for huge jaws to open and for us to be eaten like little bugs.

But that didn't happen.

When we got down under the belly, I couldn't believe it. The bottom of the monster opened up, and the arms lifted us into some kind of small room.

Hey, I thought, monsters don't have rooms. Especially metal rooms, with ladders running up the side.

The claws let go, the floor closed up beneath us, and the water started to drain out.

I tore off my mask. Zeek did the same.

"Hey, Nood!" he said. "I figured it out. This is no monster! It's a . . . well, it's a . . ." He looked at me to fill in the word.

"Submarine?"

"That's it. Some kind of mini-submarine."

"Yeah," I said. "Pretty exciting, no?"

"You bet!" he smiled. "But really, who's . . . "

Krrreeekkk! The hatchway at the top of the ladder started to turn. It flipped open.

A face poked through the hole.

"You boys okay?"

"Mrs. Emerson!" Zeek and I shouted together. "Boy, are we glad to see you!" We started jumping up and down.

Then Mr. Emerson, the other half of the famous husband-and-wife exploring team, stuck his head down. "Noodle! Zeek! Come on. We've got a job to do!"

We were up the ladder in a flash.

"We saw you boys a little while ago," Mrs. Emerson said. "But we had to dive before the big wave came."

"Yeah, the Golden Crest almost sank our surfboard," Zeek said. I nodded.

When we got to the small control room, we were amazed at all the computer screens, dials, switches, and other under-water equipment.

"This is incredible!" I said. "How long have you had this cool sub?"

"We've been looking for the wreck of Captain May's ship for a long time," Mr. Emerson said. "We finally located it on sonar."

"And we've just finished mapping it with laser photography," Mrs. Emerson said, pointing to one of the built-in computer screens. "This shows a com-plete picture of the wreck."

"Wow!" Zeek said. "Tech stuff! I love it."

I cracked a smile.

But Mrs. Emerson frowned. "Then

these looters came along and started blasting for treasure. Now this rock ledge is weak. Look at this!"

She showed us another screen with lots of squiggly lines on it. "If we don't raise this ship soon, the whole ledge will crash down and destroy it."

"Raise it?" Zeek said, his eyes going wide. "How are you going to raise that old wreck?"

"By placing balloons in the hull and inflating them," Mr. Emerson said. "This control here . . ."

"But, listen," I cried. "There isn't going to be any wreck, any us, or any Mayville unless we stop these maniacs! Look!"

One of the screens flickered in front of us.

"There they are!" I shouted.

The picture was hazy, but we could see the Boss, Baldy, and Silver-Hair dropping bundles of dynamite into a small hatchway in the wreck.

Mr. Emerson looked at Mrs. Emerson.

"Noodle's right. We've got to stop that blast." He pulled on a pair of oxygen tanks.

"Sorry, Mr. E.," I said. "We've been through that wreck. The passages are so tight only a kid could get through in the time we've got. Zeek will place the balloons. I'll go after the dynamite."

"No, boys," Mr. Emerson said. "You can't do this. We can't let you. It's much too—"

Suddenly Zeek jumped.

"That's it! That's the word! Finally, someone's going to say it! Sure, it's been different. And fun. And exciting. But it just got officially—*dangerous*!"

Zeek snapped his fingers and punched his thumb in the air. He grinned a big grin at me.

"Noodle, this is incredible. I place the balloons, you do the dynamite. What could be better? Holy cow, I can't believe it took all day to get dangerous!"

TEN

"Listen carefully, Noodle." Mr. Emerson frowned and looked right at me. I gulped.

"The dynamite will be connected to a detonator box by four colored wires. Usually red, green, yellow, and blue."

"Simple," Zeek said, nodding at me. He was feeling great.

"You must disconnect all the wires carefully," Mr. Emerson continued.

"Yeah. Or, like, *Boom!*" Zeek added, laughing.

I didn't laugh back at him.

I couldn't believe I had said I would do the dynamite.

"Don't worry," said Zeek. "It's a cinch

placing these balloons." He held a bunch of flat rubber sausages. "As soon as I finish, I'll be there for the big moment!"

"Yeah?" But I was starting to hate my plan. "And, Noodle." Mrs. Emerson said. "If that ledge starts to break apart, you get out of there!"

Great, I thought. Can you make it any more dangerous?

We climbed down into the water chamber.

Fwump! The hatch closed.

Water jetted in and the bottom slid open. We dropped out into the water. *Blub. Blub.*

Zeek swam off to the front of the wreck with a pack of those party balloons. He waved at me.

Me, the bomb expert.

I waved back.

I took a closer look at the ledge. It was like a giant stone shelf. It's going to collapse any second, Mrs. Emerson said. Yeah, just my luck. . . .

Rrrrrr! I looked up. The motorboat roared away. Okay. There was no time to spare.

I squeezed through the little hatchway. It was a tight fit, all right. No way could Mr. or Mrs. E. have done this.

I looked around. There it was, in the shimmering blue water. A pile of long ugly sticks.

There were the four wires running from the sticks to a humming black box. That was the detonator, the thing that actually triggered the blast.

Simple, Zeek had said.

Yeah, right! I'd seen enough movies to know that if I pulled the wires out the wrong way the whole thing would blow.

Something rumbled overhead. I poked my head up through the hatch.

Crrraaacckkk! A rock rolled off the ledge and crashed onto the hull. Another fell. Then another.

The ledge was cracking!

I dove back in the hatch. I looked at the

wires. This was it. Do or die. I had to start.

Pick a color, any color. Eenie-meenie-meinie— Something in my head said— green! Yes, I'll pull the green wire first!

But just as I reached for the green wire, the cabin door burst open and bubbles filled the tiny room.

It was Zeekie! He raced over to help.

But he swam in too fast and slammed into my oxygen tank.

I couldn't believe it! Clutzy thing number three!

I fell forward. I grabbed for something to catch my balance.

Riiip!

I stared at my hand.

I was holding the black box.

And all the wires were dangling from it!

ELEVEN

*K*A *BOOM!* (I thought).

But I was wrong.

Nothing happened.

Well, not really nothing. The black box stopped humming. That was good. And bubbles fizzled out of it. That was good too.

Then bubbles started to fizzle out of Zeek's mouth.

Blub. Blub. Was he saying something?

No. I think he was laughing.

And he gave me the okay sign.

Suddenly, I had to laugh too. I couldn't believe I had done the dynamite. And we were all still alive!

Zeek did a little touchdown wiggle. I tried to jump, but underwater it's hard.

Bam! Another rock smashed down on the hull.

Okay, so all our troubles weren't over.

"Hurry!" I bubbled.

Zeek popped his head out of the hatch and waved at the sub. The Emersons answered with a quick flash of the search-lights.

Suddenly, we could hear hissing from below. Clouds of bubbles rose up through the water. Zeek's balloons were filling up!

We squeezed out of the hatch and onto the deck.

Then, right before our eyes, the wrecked ship, the ship of Captain John May, founder of Mayville, started to move. For the first time in more than two hundred years!

Whoosh! The hull cleared the ledge. It tilted upright in the water and started to rise. We grabbed on to the old ship's rigging and held on for the ride.

It was amazing. We stared at each other.

We were going to the surface. And we were going in style!

Sploosh! The ship broke the surface. Water sloshed over the deck and down the sides of the hull. The old wooden planks gleamed in the sun. We tore off our masks.

"Zeekie!" I shouted.

"Noodle!" he yelled.

"WE DID IT!"

The huge ship rocked gently in the water.

But we still had one more big job to do.

"The motorboat!" I yelled. "They're getting away!"

Zeek smiled big. "Attaaack!"

We grabbed a couple of rigging ropes and jumped.

Fwing! Through a hail of stun darts, we

swooped down on the enemy ship. We both yelled out the same thing—

"DAAANNGGGERR GUUUYS!"

It was incredible!

We landed hard and acted fast.

Splash! I knocked Silver-Hair straight into the water. Mustache went all pale when he saw Zeek. He toppled over in a dead faint.

Then Baldy rushed Zeek, and the Boss turned on me. Her face got red. Boy, was she mad!

"If I can't have the treasure, nobody can!" she yelled. She hit the radio detonator button hard.

Click. She hit it again and again. *Click, click.*

"Is this what you're looking for?" I held up the black box with the colored wires. I smiled at her.

"Why, you little . . . " She picked up a dart gun, and my smile faded. She aimed it right at me.

Suddenly, that strange shadow passed

over the boat. The Boss looked up.

I threw the box at her just as she pulled the trigger.

Pwing! The dart went wild. It hit the motor, knocked it dead, bounced off the windshield, and hit Baldy right in the behind. He stiffened and plopped on his face.

Zeek and I leaped for the Boss. But she dove before we got to her.

"She's getting away!" I shouted.

Just then, a giant iron arm burst from the water. It grabbed her and hoisted her into the air.

"Hooray!" we yelled.

The mini-sub surfaced, and Mr. and Mrs. Emerson poked out their heads. "Well done, boys. The Coast Guard is on its way. We'll take over from here."

"Well, Noodle," Zeek said, looking around. "I guess that about wraps it up. All we have to do now is figure out how to get back to shore."

But I saw something flash above us,

and I started to smile. "Zeek, I think our ride is here."

We looked up. That strange shadow was passing over us again.

"You mean . . . ?"

"That's right, Zeek, old pal. The tree house roof! It's been circling the island on the hot air currents. All we have to do is reach up, and—!"

It was late in the afternoon. The sun was orange in the sky. The wind was ruffling our hair. We were soaring a hundred feet up.

Zeek turned to me, smiling. "Hey, Noodle, I thought you didn't like heights, and I didn't like water. What happened?"

"Simple, Zeek. We don't like them because we're afraid of the danger, right?"

"Yeah, I guess so."

"But the more dangerous it is, the more we like it. Because we're, well, you know . . . "

"Yeah." Then Zeek said, "Noodle? Is

there anything we can't do?"

I thought about that. I looked back at the island. The old ship was riding high on the waves.

"No," I said. "I can't think of anything."

I smiled a wide smile and punched my thumb in the air. Zeek did the same.

Wrong move. Double clutzy wrong move.

We both lost our grip on the glider.

We dropped! *Umph!*

Luckily, it was only a ten-foot drop.

Even more luckily, we dropped on soft sand.

Even incredibly more luckily, we dropped on our own beach blanket, right next to my mom and dad!

We landed in a heap.

My mom turned away from her magazine and smiled. My dad woke up.

"Oh," he said. "It must be time to leave. Sorry you kids are having such a boring weekend."

Zeek slapped my arm and grinned at me.

"It's okay, Mr. N., " Zeek said. "We found something to do."

"Something different," I said.

"Yeah, something fun.

"Exciting," I said.

"Yeah, and even a little . . ."

Have you read the other dangerous adventures of . . .

It all begins when Noodle and Zeek go to check out a new adventure store. Little do they know that a simple shopping trip will lead to a cave with kidnapped explorers and stolen treasure in DANGER GUYS.

In DANGER GUYS BLAST OFF, our heroes are off for a day at the Mayville carnival. Until their rocket ride goes haywire, and they discover their mad science teacher is planning to blow up Mayville School. . . .

DANGER GUYS: HOLLYWOOD HALLOWEEN finds Noodle and Zeek making a movie of their own. But lightning strikes, and they are suddenly among giant dinosaurs and sword-fighting skeletons who aren't exactly in the script.